Tickle the Tasmanian Devil

Susannah McFarlane   Lachlan Creagh

A Scholastic Australia Book

This is Tom and his friends—
Toby, Tilly, Tahlia and Tim.

Tom is terribly ticklish, the most ticklish of all the Tasmanian devils in Tassie.

Tom has been ticklish since he was a toddler.

Even now, just one tiny tickle and
Tom begins to titter.

Tom is terrifically topsy-turvy when
Tilly tickles him on the trampoline.

Tom twists and turns when Toby tickles
him while eating tagliatelle at teatime.

And Tom totally takes off if his
toes or tummy are tickled.
(That's Tim and Tahlia tickling
Tom—what a tag-team!)

Then one day, one Tuesday
at twenty to two, Tom was
trying to tether a tall teepee.
It was a tad tricky!

As Tom tentatively tied a totem to the top of the teepee, a tiny tiger moth twirled in the wind and touched Tom's toes. It tickled!

Tom twitched and tried to keep on tying the totem without tumbling down the teepee.

A tea tree leaf then
twirled up and touched
Tom's tummy.

It tickled! Tom tittered, but then he began to teeter.

Tom was still being tickled and the teepee began to totter. Tom looked set to topple! It was terrible.

Then . . .

Ta-Dah!

Tim, Tahlia, Tilly and Toby all stood
on top of each other and teased
Tom by the toes and took him down
the totem pole.

What terrific teamwork!

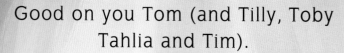

Good on you Tom (and Tilly, Toby
Tahlia and Tim).

What about you?
Are you ticklish too?